WITHDRAWN

This SCRIBBLERS

book belongs to:

....

Stratford Upon Avon Literary Festival Salariya Picture Book Prize

The Salariya Book Company partnered with the Stratford-upon-Avon Literary Festival to launch a prize to find the next big children's author-illustrator. The winner would have their debut picture book published by Salariya.

Luna and the Moon Rabbit was selected from the final shortlist of titles to win the prize.

The judges:

Annie Ashworth is the Director of the Stratford-Upon-Avon Literary Festival.

Nick Butterworth is a children's author and illustrator who has sold more than 15 million books worldwide, including the bestselling *Percy the Park Keeper* series.

Jodie Hodges is a children's literary agent at United Agents.

David Salariya is a designer, author and the founder and Managing Director of The Salariya Book Company and its imprints Bookhouse, Scribblers and Scribo.

Ashley King is an illustrator and bookseller at Waterstones.

Tereze Brikmane is a bookseller at the multi-award-winning Tales on Moon Lane bookshop.

Sarah McIntyre is an acclaimed writer and illustrator of children's picture books and comics.

About the author and illustrator: Camille Whitcher is a graduate of the Cambridge School of Art and the first winner of the Stratford-Salariya Children's Picture Book Prize.

This edition published in Great Britain in MMXVIII by Scribblers, an imprint of The Salariya Book Company Ltd 25 Marlborough Place, Brighton BN1 1UB www.salariya.com

SALARIYA
SCRIBO BOOK HOUSE SCRIBBLERS

Text & illustrations © Camille Whitcher MMXVIII
© The Salariya Book Company Ltd MMXVIII

HB ISBN-13: 978-1-912233-25-0

1 3 5 7 9 8 6 4 2

A CIP catalogue record for this book is available from the British Library.

Printed and bound in China

Printed on paper from sustainable sources

All rights reserved. No part of this publication may be reproduced, stored in or introduced into a retrieval system or transmitted in any form, or by any means (electronic, mechanical, photocopying, recording or otherwise) without the written permission of the publisher. Any person who does any unauthorised act in relation to this publication may be liable to criminal prosecution and civil claims for damages.

This book is sold subject to the conditions that it shall not, by way of trade or otherwise, be lent, resold, hired out, or otherwise circulated without the publisher's prior consent in any form or binding or cover other than that in which it is published and without similar condition being imposed on the subsequent purchaser.

Visit
www.salariya.com
for our online catalogue and
free fun stuff.

Luna
and the
Moon
Rabbit

by camille
whitcher

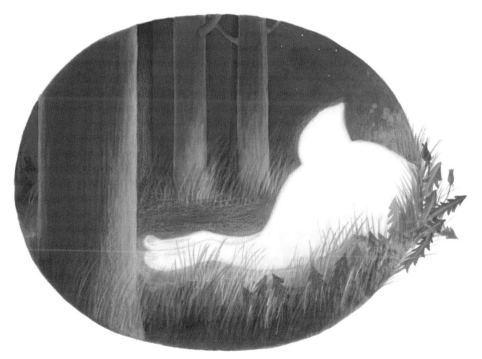

SCRIBBLERS
a SALARIYA *imprint*

Luna was sitting with her Grandma gazing up at the bright shining Moon.

"Look up there, Luna," said Grandma pointing up, "when the Moon is full and the sky is clear, you can see him."

"See who?" asked Luna.

"Why, the Moon Rabbit, of course!" replied Grandma.

"A rabbit on the Moon? What's a rabbit doing up there?" asked Luna.

"Well, some say he spends his time pounding rice to make rice cakes, like these ones I made for us," replied Grandma. "If you offer him a rice cake, he's sure to come and visit you."

Luna stared at the Moon. She was sure that there was no such thing as a Moon Rabbit, and that he wouldn't come and visit. But still she couldn't help but wonder...

Luna's curiosity got the better of her. So she took a rice cake to her bedroom and waited and waited and...

Suddenly he arrived! "The Moon Rabbit! He's here!" Luna gasped.

Luna wasted no time. They started
off on their moonlit adventure.

Luna led the way into the magical woods.

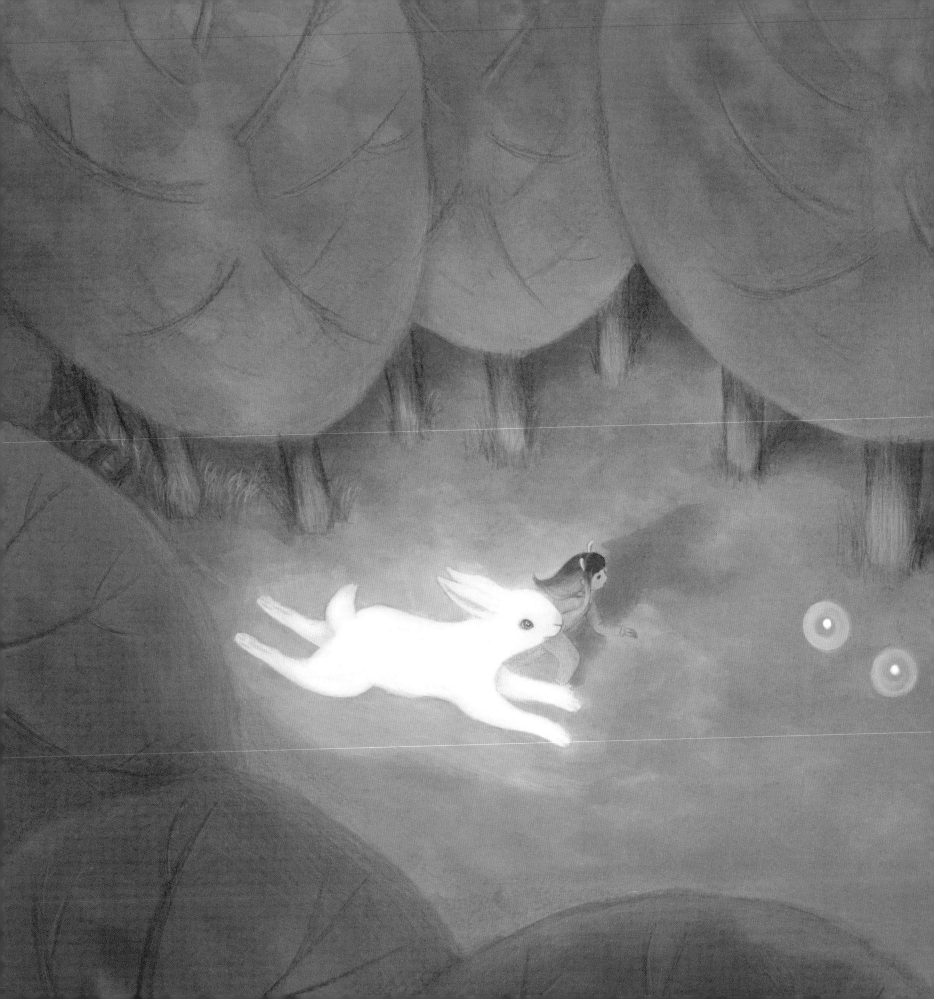

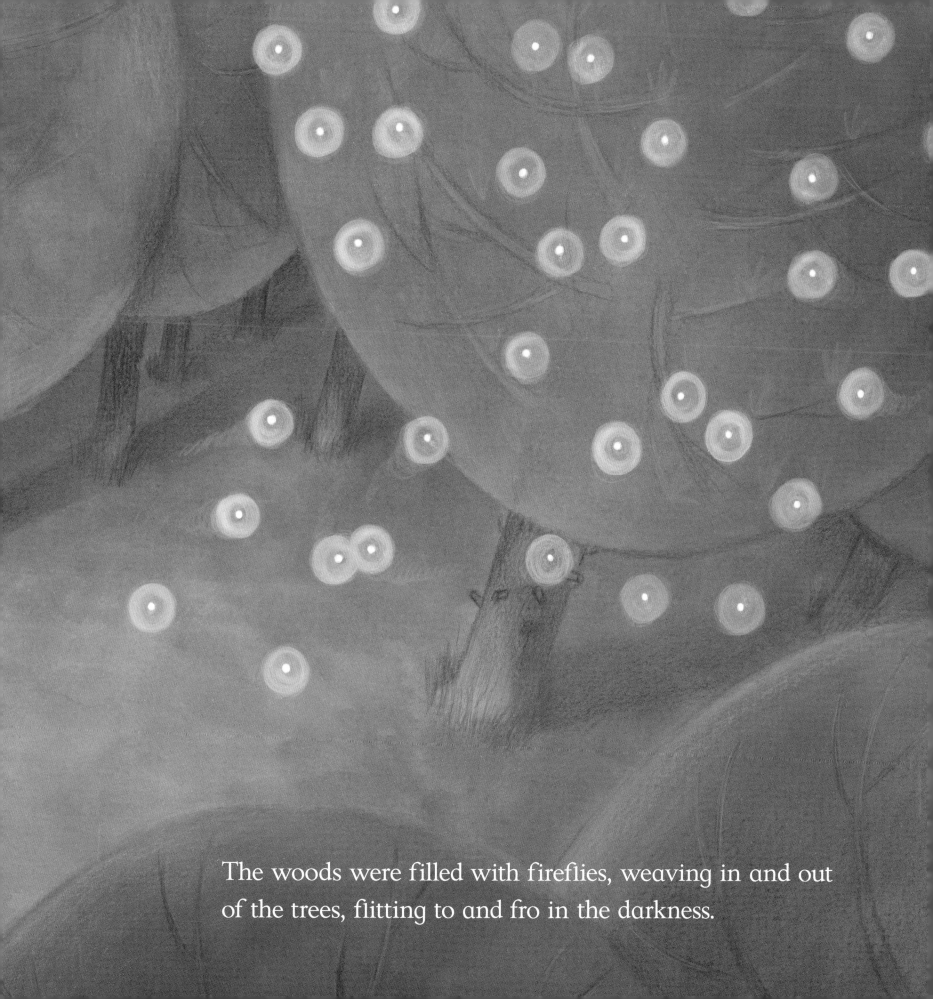

The woods were filled with fireflies, weaving in and out of the trees, flitting to and fro in the darkness.

The fireflies gathered
around a huge tree.
Luna and the Moon
Rabbit took a closer look.

Then something
caught Moon
Rabbit's attention
and off he went.

Luna tried to keep up, racing through the dark woods after him.

Where was he going?

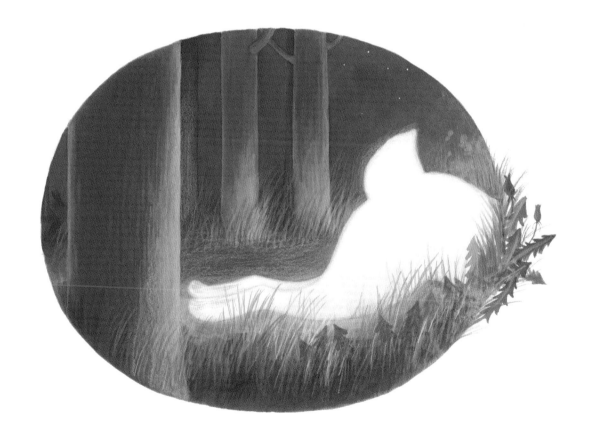

Luna soon found him munching away. "Of course!"
she thought, "the golden dandelion field. He must
be hungry. But why are the dandelions opening up
at night?"

Standing among the swaying flowers, Moon Rabbit gave her a dandelion.

She held it gently when, all of a sudden, the petals started twisting and turning, transforming into a fluffy, cottony, glowing ball.

Luna blew away the glowing seeds
and they were picked up and swirled
around by the gentle, warm breeze,

joining the stars in the night sky.

Luna sat with her new friend watching the twinkling night sky, every so often wishing upon a star.

As Moon Rabbit sat twitching his nose, Luna wondered if he too was making wishes.

Down at the river, they watched
the koi gently swimming and
swirling in the rippling water.

Swish, swish, swish.
Around and around.
Luna yawned and her eyes began to close.

With Luna on his back, Moon Rabbit hopped through the woods, until Luna's home was in sight.

Moon Rabbit tucked a heavy-eyed
and sleepy Luna into bed.

Luna wanted to tell Moon Rabbit to come back
again, but the words melted into her dreams.

Twitching his nose, Moon Rabbit headed off back home. Would he be back to see Luna again?

She was sure he would.